19.95

DATE DUE

SONG OF THE SUN

Auh nicnocuecuexantia in nepapan ahuiac xochitl.
I fill my cloak with precious flowers.
                                        Aztec lyric fragment

For Henry Thompson
—M. L.

Song of the Sun is based on an unnamed myth included in *Historia Eclesiástica Indiana*. Transcribed for Gerónimo de Mendieta in the 1600s. Mexico: Antigua Libreria, 1870. The song fragment is from "Cuica Peuhcayotl," translated to Spanish from the Nahuatl by Cecilio A. Robelo. Cuauhnahuac: 1900. Included in *Cantares en Idioma Mexicano* manuscript. Mexico: Oficina Tipografica de la Secretaria de Fomento, 1904.

This myth is from the Aztec of Mexico.

ILLUSTRATIONS © Charles Reasoner

Library of Congress Cataloging-in-Publication Data

Lilly, Melinda.
   Song of the sun / retold by Melinda Lilly;   illustrated by Charles Reasoner.
      p. cm.—(Latin American tales and myths)
   Summary: Eagle Warrior tries to find a way to free his fellow musicians who have been captured by the jealous Sun because they have only honored the Spirit of Night.
   ISBN 1-57103-267-3
   1. Aztecs—Folklore. 2. Aztec mythology. 3. Tales—Mexico. [1. Aztecs—Folklore. 2. Indians of Mexico—Folklore. 3. Folklore—Mexico.] I. Reasoner, Charles, ill. II. Title III. Series: Lilly, Melinda. Latin American tales and myths.
F1219.76.F65L55 1999
398.2'0972—dc21   98–10321
                                                           CIP
                                                           AC

Printed in the USA

Latin American Tales and Myths

SONG OF THE SUN

An Aztec Myth

Retold by
Melinda Lilly

Illustrated by
Charles Reasoner

The Rourke Press, Inc.
Vero Beach, Florida 32964

Eagle Warrior awakened before dawn. He arose silently, listening to the music of Night: the deep even breathing of his fellow musicians, the water lapping at the banks of the canals outside, and the soft hooting of an owl.

"Great Owl, Night's companion," he murmured, picking up his clay flute. "I am ready to honor your lord and mine, Tezcatlipoca, the Spirit of Night." He lit a stick of incense and set it in the burner on the windowsill, eager for the ceremony of Night to begin. He had practiced for years as one at the end of a line, thinking his flute's voice could never be heard among so many. This time, Eagle Warrior had been honored by being chosen by Spirit of Night to lead in the temple ceremony and he hoped his music would be pleasing.

Eagle Warrior woke the other music makers. "Owl has spoken. Night calls," he whispered in the firelight. "It's time to go to the temple."

The musicians arranged themselves into groups as they gathered at the Temple of Night. The dancers stilled their rattles. Conch shell players lifted their instruments and listened to the faraway ocean. The musicians with whistles and flutes stood in readiness, their eyes fixed on Eagle Warrior as he stepped forward to the steady beats of the *vevetl* and *teponaztli* drums. Cradling his flute in his arms, Eagle Warrior climbed the temple's stone steps to the carved room on top.

Eagle Warrior lowered his plumed head and entered the small, smoky room. Long ago, it was Spirit of Night who had brought music and color to his people by playing a flute. Now Eagle Warrior could hardly wait to offer him the same gifts.

He moved to the window and looked out. At the base of the pyramid, four sharp whistles signaled the start of the dance. The conch shells, rattles, whistles, and the other flute players joined the drums in praising Tezcatlipoca. The singers chanted the many names of their lord: Spirit of Night, Soul of the World, the Ever Present and Ever Near.

Closing his eyes, Eagle Warrior lifted his flute and began his song. With each breath, he could feel Night filling him with power. With each note Eagle Warrior filled the world with song and joy. He played as he had never played before.

His music soared up to the sky followed by his gaze. The eyes of Night looked back at him, watching as stars—the lord Tezcatlipoca was listening. Eagle Warrior and his friends serenaded the Spirit of Night as the sky began to brighten with daylight.

In the House of Dawn, Tonatiuh Sun stirred from his rest, also hearing the songs of Night. He listened to the incomparable beauty of Eagle Warrior's flute, but the music brought him no pleasure. It was not for him. Again he'd awakened to Night's song, Night's praises. "What's Night, but cold and colorless," seethed Sun. "Everything draped in black!" Sun burned hot with jealousy. His flames pierced the morning sky. "I bring warmth and light, but do they thank me? If they care nothing for my gifts, I'll take away the music and color and keep them for myself!"

Blazing, Sun hurled himself at the remaining darkness. In a flash, Night's stars were extinguished. Tezcatlipoca the Night disappeared from Earth to the dead lands below.

From the temple, Eagle Warrior watched Sun's rays reach across the land like hungry fingers. Hungry for praise, song, and color. Eagle Warrior's flute sounded a warning, but it was too late. Sun scooped up the musicians and trapped them in his clenched fists.

"Sing songs for me!" he commanded in a roaring voice. "You praise Night, but have forgotten Day! Without my light and warmth there would be no color, no music, no life! What is Night without Day?"

Safe in the temple room, only Eagle Warrior had escaped Sun's grasp. Shading his eyes and squinting, he saw and heard his friends trying to break free. The drummers pounded Sun's palms. Feathered dancers kicked his curving fingers. Rattles shook furiously. Flutes cried. Conch shells blared, trying to blast a way out of their prison. Singers sang of their lost homes.

Sun didn't notice his prisoners' struggles or sorrow. He basked in the beauty of their music and color, but remained unsatisfied. The songs were still not for him. He tightly laced his fingers together to keep the music and color from escaping. Gray silence descended upon the world.

Eagle Warrior looked away from Sun and down at the land, now bleached by harsh morning light. His friends were gone. Music, color, and laughter were no more, Sun had taken them from the world. The people who were left moved as ghosts over the faded, whispering land.

Eagle Warrior covered his eyes with his feathered shield and wept. Then, when he could cry no more, he lifted his flute. He called to the Spirit of Night with each note, asking for help in freeing his friends and bringing life back to his world.

Ninoyolnonotza, campa nicuiz yectli yan cuicatl
Ye nican ic chocan noyollo. Tezcatlipoca!
I long to find the sweet songs
My soul weeps. Tezcatlipoca!

He played his song all day with no answer from Night, but Sun heard. "One escaped! One flute still plays for Night and not Day!" he said, blazing with anger. Following the sound to the pyramid, Sun reached his fiery fingers into the temple to grab Eagle Warrior and capture his airy melody.

With an unwavering breath, Eagle Warrior cried, "Tezcatlipoca! Tezcatlipoca! Tezcatlipoca!" At last, Spirit of Night heard the call and stirred. He rose from the dead world. Spreading his black, star-studded cloak across the sky, he plunged Eagle Warrior into the safety of darkness as Sun dove below the horizon, clutching his captives.

13

On his flute of stars, Spirit of Night blew forth a melody like a cool wind. "You are the only music maker left in the world," his flute sang to Eagle Warrior. "You must find the House of Dawn and offer your gifts to Tonatiuh Sun. He is hungry. Only when you and all the people honor him as you've honored me will he free his prisoners." The wind stilled as Spirit of Night turned and disappeared into the evening sky.

Eagle Warrior left his city, searching for the House of Dawn. He wandered the wet forest and the desert. He climbed the mountains, scaling the rocks and old lava flows. He crossed the shifting coastal sands and came to the edge of the great sea just as Sun's first flames of daylight appeared.

He looked around for a canoe to take him across the waters, but found nothing. He ran into the waves only to be thrown back onto the beach, sputtering. With an eagle's war cry he threw himself into the air, but was more warrior than eagle and fell to the ground instead of flying. He dove into the breakers and began to swim, battered by the rough surf. The powerful waves tumbled him end over end. He struggled to the surface for air.

"Spirit of Night, help me!" he gasped as he sank again beneath the water. In the darkness of the great sea he heard the distant trill of his lord's flute, then shadowy figures surrounded him. He was lifted above the waves on the sloping back of a giant turtle. He stretched out on the living island, turning to see the slick, strong movements of a whale and an alligator swimming alongside.

"I must reach Sun," he gasped. "Before he rises too high. He has my friends, color, and music."

"You can't run there from here, Eagle Warrior," said Turtle, cocking her head.

"You can't fly there," chuckled Alligator.

"You can't swim there either," added Whale, flexing his tail.

"We will help you," offered Turtle. "We'll make a bridge to the Sun. Spirit of Night called us with his flute, commanding that it be done."

"Hurry, friends," urged Eagle Warrior. As he watched the horizon, Sun broke free of the water and began to rise into the sky.

"I am a turtle, I do not hurry," Turtle replied, planting her feet in the shallows. The three animals lined up mouth to tail, making a bridge that stretched from the shore to the water below the rising sun.

Eagle Warrior stood on Turtle's enormous back. "Tonatiuh Sun!" he called. "I am Cuauhtli Eagle Warrior! Listen to my *cuicatl*, my music! Free my brothers and sisters!" He raised his flute to his lips.

"I know you sing for Night, not to honor me!" Sun yelled, glaring.

Eagle Warrior's breath died in the flute. He couldn't play the song he had played so well the night before. Tezcatlipoca the Night was not with him. He was alone with angry Sun.

In desperation, he looked back across the living bridge to his home. There was nothing left to sing about in that gray world. His voice remained silent. Without Sun's blessings, the land was a lifeless place. For the first time Eagle Warrior saw that color, music, and life came not only from Night, but also from Day. How could he have overlooked Sun's gifts?

Taking a deep breath, he faced Tonatiuh Sun, remembering the beauty of his former world. He blew into his flute, trilling softly so only Sun could hear.

TONATIUH! TONATIUH! TONATIUH!

His music sang of sunlight sparkling on the waves. It sang of warmth and brightness and of light shining through the clouds.

Hearing his name spoken with reverence, Sun listened. Eagle Warrior played sweetly, thanking Sun for the rays warming him.

TONATIUH! TONATIUH! TONATIUH!

With each breath, Eagle Warrior soothed Sun.

24

Music spread across the sky. Sun loosened his fists. Listening, the musicians at last were able to see the House of Dawn not as a prison, but as the place where life begins each morning. They joined Eagle Warrior in celebrating the sunrise.

TONATIUH! TONATIUH! TONATIUH!

The people of the world lifted their heads, looking up from the colorless, silent land. Their eyes fixed on Sun, spinning in the sky like a festival of warmth, light, and life.

TONATIUH! TONATIUH! TONATIUH!

They sang, thanking him. The sky and Earth echoed with Sun's praise.

Sun listened to the wondrous sound of his own name and was filled with joy. At last the people sang for him! Sunlight twirled around him and he danced, chanting along with his people.

TONATIUH! TONATIUH! TONATIUH!

27

His hands stretched out to free his music makers and embrace the world.

The musicians leaped onto Whale's back. They danced along the living bridge, playing notes made of the hues of daylight: red, blue, yellow, green.

TONATIUH! TONATIUH! TONATIUH!

The world sang. Color filled heaven and Earth once again. Lifted by song, Eagle Warrior flew with Sun through the sky to the House of Dusk, scattering music and joy. On the western shore, Eagle Warrior's flute sang to his people and all creation joined in the dance for Day and for Night. Listening, Tonatiuh and Tezcatlipoca swirled together in the sky, mingling their colors into the light and dark radiance of evening.

PRONUNCIATION AND DEFINITION GUIDE

Aztec (AZ tek) — a powerful civilization of ancient Mexico; also called the Mexica

conch shell (KONK SHEL) — A large, spiral shell found in tropical oceans, it can be used as a horn or in jewelry.

Cuauhtli (KWAW tlee) — the name of an Aztec warrior

cuicatl (kwee KAHT l) — Nahuatl for song

Nahuatl (nah WAHT l) — the language of the Aztecs, still spoken in some areas of Mexico; written Nahuatl uses pictures to represent ideas and sounds.

teponaztli drum (teh poh NAZ tlee DRUM) — A carved, two-tone, wooden gong of the Aztecs. It is played with rubber-tipped drum sticks.

Tezcatlipoca (tess kah tlee POH kah) — Supreme god and symbol of night, he wore a smoking mirror on his foot that showed him everything that was happening in the world.

Tonatiuh (toh nah TEE wuh) — Sun god and the guiding spirit of warriors, his name means, "He who goes forth shining."

vevetl drum (weh WET l DRUM) — a carved, wooden, upright drum of the Aztecs; the solemn, deep sound of big vevetl drums could be heard as far away as six miles (10 kilometers). Smaller vevetl drums were hung around the neck to enable dancing.